SAMMAR

Eldon Crowe

Tellwell Talent
www.tellwell.ca

ISBN
978-0-2288-1373-6 (Paperback)

I

The moment he stood upon the threshold, it came back to him. He was once more stumbling to the ground on his stomach, ignominiously, his sword clanging hard upon the old, cracked flagstones of the Mestian Way. Once more, he was twisting his body around, cat-like, searching for his opponent but perceiving the over-tardiness of the movement. The knowledge that the other man's blade was already flashing down in a savage arc through the air toward him froze him once more as it had at that moment. He winced in the dark as he was once again cut deeply and clean to the bone between the right thigh and hip, where his armour was jointed. Agony, stark and livid, stabbed through his leg and shot up through his abdomen just as it had then.

He had tasted blood as he had tried to bite down on the pain but he had known he would be dead after the follow-up blow, no longer having the strength or good fortune to deflect it. Sammos, in his great wisdom, had withdrawn his favour from him and had decreed that he should die.

But the Emperor had cried, *'Hold!'* and, just like that, his opponent had put up his blade. And so he had been saved. Yet saved ignobly.

Agriabus stood, swallowing, his head still in the memory. He shook it and involuntarily drew his surcoat tighter about himself, peering into the gloom. His breath came dry and ragged from his lungs. He was standing just inside the heavy iron doors of the vast, high chamber but he could see only shadows within.

'*Have to keep it together. The City needs me. He needs me. Even if I was unable to defend his honour – or that of Sammar.*'

A great emptiness hung all about him that was somehow not empty but rather filled with dim, writhing spirits. He shuddered. The great god of Sammar's dwelling place was ever dark and gloomy, as he and all Sammkites knew, its pall of sacrificial smoke stultifying, and yet he wondered to himself if any other citizen of the Empire were quite as familiar with its dread as he was. '*How can my Master think in here let alone pray for the City – if, in fact, that is what he has been doing in here all this time. Yet, he is here in this place and I am Prefect of the Purple of the Glorious City. I should not fear the Shrine of Sammos, yet I swear I love it not.*'

Reluctantly, he stepped into the holy place. In the dryness, the pain throbbing in his right leg where Sulcharek's blade had made the vicious cut, he began slowly to make his way across the smooth marble tiles of the Shrine. '*It was three weeks ago when he struck me. I do not believe it has been that long.*' He snorted. Even the royal women, including the Imperial Consort, herself, the Lady Gedalia of Issus, had not yet been sent from the City when his son had spoken his treacherous words. It had been shameful even to *think* such a thing then, let alone utter it aloud! '*Yes, and now he is one of* them, *isn't he – an enemy of Sammar.*'

Agriabus trembled with fury as he limped across the floor, his high boots snicking upon the marble. He could still see Sulcharek's face before him, floating in the shadows, so proud and haughty and full of treachery, advocating the abandonment of Sammkos in order to declare it a free and open city. '*And now I know that it was to present it as a gift to his new Master, the Great and Sublime Krahl - when he should deign to enter it with his begrimed boots. PAH!*'

The van of the Odrum armies had still been warring in Pentes then. The Krahl himself had been still far to the east of the Mare Nubium with his main host. Agriabus had been so insulted by Sulcharek's plan, that he had gone beyond endurance and had impulsively drawn his blade from its scabbard in the Emperor's very presence…..

Agriabus sighed deeply in the dark vault and the sound made the hairs on his neck stand on end. The torches held in high iron sconces fastened into the stone walls scarcely illuminated the great arched vault of the ceiling high above him. Ahead now, he could make out a flickering red-orange glow - the burning Altar of Sammos near the far wall of the Shrine.

'Perhaps it is fitting that my liege lord has decided to remain here these seven days, since the siege of the City became like a tightly cinched noose. And I am obliged to come here, aren't I? Oh yes, for apart from the holy Priests of the Purple no-one now but me, poor Agriabus, the son of a low-born Outlander from Pentes, is permitted to look upon the Emperor's face on pain of death.'

Finally, the Altar stood before him, wide and squat and deep and crouching upon the ground like a monstrous brazier. Its flames welled upward in a blazing inferno toward the open ceiling of the Eastern Apse of the Shrine directly above it. A Purple Priest stood near to it in his flowing robes, chanting in Ancient Scala, which had always sounded harsh and angry to Agriabus. He was flinging mulchak fat onto its sacred fire and the Altar hissed like a living, breathing creature. Tall torches burned at its sides and behind it, carved into the very stone of the high wall itself by Sammkite stonemasons ages past, towered the statue of Sammos himself, twenty feet high and draped in immense white robes trimmed with the Divine Purple.

Agriabus saw the god of Sammar emerge from the gloom behind the Altar and shuddered. The divine likeness was fearsome to behold, especially when the flickering light of the flames was upon it, and Agriabus always averted his eyes from the awesome face whenever he was obliged to come beneath its gaze. He knew that the immense eyes were sightless yet defiant, the curls of the hair upturned like daggers' blades beneath the circlet upon the divine brow, the wide mouth twisted in an almost lecherous sneer.

Agriabus lowered his eyes deliberately to Sammos's giant feet where, standing serenely like angels, the sculpted likenesses of the Emperor's revered forebears, Gotshalk and Nemurra, first Emperor and Empress of Sammar, stood. The great god's massive hands lay protectively upon their heads and they were each carved, it was said, according to their height and appearance in life. Their faces bore all of the regal stateliness and dignity that Agriabus had been taught had been borne by all Sammkite Emperors and Empresses; ever since the Holy Empire of Sammar itself had risen from the ashes of the eastern part of the colossal Realm of Scala in Ancient Days.

Before the Altar, in the shifting light of its fire, sat a bare, flat couch. Agriabus beheld the form of a man slouched upon it.

At once, he banished all else from his mind and hurried forward. He came and knelt, painfully, upon the stone floor on his left knee before the man.

"My Lord," he intoned, gravely, using the deep, steady voice used at Court and, bowing his head, he waited. The silence of the Shrine and the crackling of the sacred fire were all that came to his ears and after a short while he raised his head and lifted his eyes to the couch.

Callimach XI, Emperor of Sammar, sat upon his simple, austere seat, the writhing firelight of the Altar giving his face a ghoulish pallor. His sunken eyes were closed and his lips were tightly drawn and pressed together as if they masked a great pain deep within. His long, dark hair was loose and unkempt and his body, once solid and proud, now seemed shrunken and frail. He wore no imperial circlet upon his brow and Agriabus saw that he was garbed only in a thin shift of coarse linen. It was the garb of a Sammkite Penitent.

Agriabus winced in spite of himself. The Emperor looked to his eyes as a wraith and no more. *'We are doomed. O Sammos the Great and Dreadful, we are assuredly doomed if this be the condition of my Master. Callimach the Firewind! He who swept the rebellious armies of his odious uncle, the treacherous Duke of Sinlok, from my own remote province of Pentes only eighteen months past- before the Deluge came. He who rode and fought like the windstorm, pinning Sinlok himself against an alder tree with a mighty throw of his javelin. Can this really be him? Protect and Defend him and us, O Divine!'*

"Sire," Agriabus whispered, forcing his lips to move and air to come from his lungs, "I bring you the morn's report. Today, by the light of dawn, it is revealed that the situation in the Mestian Quarter is now critical. The Dalcos-by-the-Sea has suffered damage, which the Lord Tistertich has termed 'unsustainable.' He has sent me word that two of the Four Walls are now in dire peril of a breach and that Odrum tunnels are undermining the other two. Lantass has slipped back into the City and reports that the massive Odrum Fire-Tube has been spotted in the Forest far beyond the West Wall and that the Krahl's war galleys have overcome the last of the allied sloops of war in the Golden Lake but yester-eve. His fleet has now closed the Strait of Jaas to the South. The ravaged Stenican and Parrian fleets, My Lord, have put out to Sea far behind the Strait now and are withdrawing to home waters. The Ladrian galleases to the North in the Mare Nubium continue to sit uselessly behind the great and infernal Odrum breakwater Chains blocking the Run leading into the Golden Lake itself. It is now only - " Agriabus felt a spasm suddenly tighten his throat, cutting off his words, but he forced himself to continue " – now only a matter of …. Sire, the defenders on the Dalcos in the Mestian Quarter have fallen under the direct attack of volleys from the guns of the Odrum fleet in the Golden Lake!" He stopped, trying to keep himself from choking shamefully with tears in his Master's presence.

Helplessly, he looked at the man slumped upon the couch before the Altar. Long silent minutes fell on them like tiny, dead leaves falling from a leaden sky; falling and then passing forever away.

Then Callimach spoke. "I know what else you would say, Agriabus, were you not an honourable man and incapable of uttering the words in my presence," he said, in a hollow voice so weak and brittle and desolate that it pained Agriabus to hear it, "You would tell me that the breaching of the Sea Wall is imminent and that all hasty efforts to staunch the wound by the City Watch and the soldiers of the Mestian Citadel by erecting earthen ramparts before it will delay its fate not a whit. You would tell me that our remaining allies, Stenna and Parr and Ladris, who had all aligned themselves with us only so long as we could benefit their expanding trade against that of Odrum – which we can no longer - have been permanently cut off from us. You would tell me that they would no longer come to our aid even if they were not cut off from us and, lastly, you would observe that the Blasphemer, himself, with his minions arrayed about him will soon enter this Glorious City – this City which has withstood countless Pagan onslaughts for a thousand years and whose Walls have never fallen to any enemy. All of that is what else you would say were your lips capable of doing so, is it not?"

The Emperor turned his tired, bleary eyes toward Agriabus and the Prefect felt tears welling in his own eyes as he returned their empty gaze. "Yes, Sire," Agriabus gasped, "I would tell you all of those things but I would also tell you that the soldiers and merchants and peasants – all those who have fled into the City before those cruel advances, by both land and sea, which the Krahl has launched and which have destroyed their homes and have desecrated the sacred provinces of the Holy Empire - *all* of them, great and small, need to see their Lord and to have him in their midst at this time of dread so that they might take strength and comfort from the sight of his face. You cannot remain in this place overlong, My Lord. You *must* go out into the City. Before it is too late. Please!"

The Emperor shifted on his hard, bare seat. "The First Priest has brought the Censer of burning coals out into the streets of the City and is traversing the Four Quarters," he said, shortly, returning his eyes to the flames, "The people will see therein the sacred smoke and smell the blessings of Sammos. Therein is their strength and comfort to be gotten. I, myself, will remain here for I have set votive candles." He raised his arm and pointed a gnarled finger over-top of the Altar without lifting his gaze from the fire. "Behold them, there, between the divine feet and also before the likeness of the Empress, whose beauty and courage have never been matched by any highborn Sammkite lady since the day of her death and whose pure spirit may yet render us aid from Sammos' Blessed Beyond." He looked round, sharply, at Agriabus. "Do you not see the garb I wear? I have much of which to repent and of which you are ignorant. Do not bother me now with endless words concerning matters the outcome of which Sammos, in his great wisdom, has already decided."

Agriabus, in anguish, turned and looked up at the fair and noble face of the Empress Nemurra, which in truth he had always considered the only agreeable feature of this dark and daunting place. He tried to recall all of the Epics and Sagas composed in her honour. It was a thousand years past, he knew, when she, but a maiden when suffering under the atrocities committed by the Western Barbarians who had completed the destruction of Scala - and witnessing therein the rapes and murders of her sisters and mother - had asked, upon wedding Gotschalk and becoming Empress of the New Empire, for the leader of those responsible to be brought before her and her husband as they sat in judgment upon their thrones.

It was said that she had arisen from her throne, snatched the unsheathed sword from the Emperor's very lap and had, herself, plunged it into the Barbarian leader's breast to its very hilt. Gotschalk, seeing his tender wife do this thing in front of him, had been struck dumb with amazement and admiration. *'Would she were here now! But, perhaps, in truth, her boldness Beyond can still help the Empire and even steel the Emperor's blood as well.'*

"Sire," said Agriabus, turning back to his master, "I am sure that the spirit of the Empress looks with favour upon the City and that Sammos himself is not unmindful of its plight."

Callimach grunted and turned and gazed at the fire of the Altar once more. The Purple Priest flung more fat into its flames and there came a great seething from it. Agriabus shook with a dark dread as he heard it and the feeling of warmth that had entered into him at the sight of Nemurra's face and of the bringing to mind of her bold deeds fled his body, leaving it cold and empty once again. "Come, Agriabus," said Callimach, turning back toward him and placing his hand upon the couch beside him, "sit with me awhile. I would speak with you."

The Emperor's blue eyes, Agriabus saw as they looked at him, were shot through with red. "My Lord," he whispered, "It's not just the Dalcos Sea Wall in the Mestian Quarter but also the battered Wall in the Heratikkon …."

"I would speak with you awhile of your son, old friend. I have heard news of him. Now come. Sit."

'I have no son. I HAVE NO SON!' Agriabus began to tremble violently and passed a shaking hand across his face but he rose and went to the couch and sat down heavily beside his Master. He grimaced

as a brief spasm wracked his right leg and then gathered his robes about him, flinging them to the side of his body away from the Emperor.

"Good," Callimach whispered, "Very good. You must rest now. Grieving fathers must rest."

"But, My Lord, the City...."

"I have no sons left to me, Agriabus. Corden, my eldest, died of the Red Ague when he was still a child, my second, Callos, cruelly murdered by unholy assassins whom, I swear by Sammos, were hired by the Imperial Consort's ungrateful family. Though I will never prove that now." Agriabus felt Callimach's despairing eyes pierce him as the Emperor drew a deep breath which rattled dryly in his chest. "She never loved me, Agriabus, but only my throne. I can see that now but Sammos forgive me I love her still. Can you understand that? I know it is folly." Agriabus shifted uncomfortably on the bench in the face of his Master's anguish. "And *she*, knowing that by the ancient Laws she could not bear the title of 'Empress', has ever schemed and plotted to have her son take my Seat when I was gone. That son whom she bore the noble Duke of Halsa, my esteemed friend and counsellor before Sammos claimed him. She has bundled the boy away, Agriabus, but I know where he is. Even now I know it. He is an ungrateful whelp, my friend, a dishonour to his father and a creature of his mother's jealousies. He can never have the Throne of Sammar. He will not, not even now, not while I live, even if that be only a few hours more."

Agriabus tried to clear his throat but only coughed roughly. "Sire," he gasped, "the tragedies that have befallen your sons have affected the very Empire itself ...."

"There is no other issue of my body. Don't you see, old friend? My closest heir by the ancient Laws is my beautiful, dear niece, Callia, the Princess of Dervos. She is a girl of twelve, Agriabus. Twelve! My younger brother's only daughter and the heir to his tiny fiefdom on the Sea which, in treachery, he has declared a kingdom – even while beholding the dire peril of Sammar, the Mother. Vain fool." Callimach sighed and shook his head, sadly. "But they are a hundred leagues from here and my niece is now beyond the aid of all my arms. I have disinherited my brother, Agriabus, cut him off from the Imperial Throne - but not her. Sammos knows that should this Seat not be destroyed forthwith with my demise, it belongs to Callia of Dervos. I would give anything to ensure her crowned and enthroned in Sammkos. But my brother has become so afraid of the Krahl that in his madness to try to save her paltry inheritance of Dervos he has planned to betrothe the girl to the King of Rilesh and to smuggle the child into the uttermost barbaric north. She belongs to Sammos, Agriabus, but *they?* No. They may pay homage to Sammos with their lips but their hearts are far from him." Callimach shook his head again. "To think that all that will be left of the Name of Sammar after the end of Sammkos will be the weight of a lost Destiny on the shoulders of such a poor creature thousands of stadia from the sacred lands of her birth. I cannot bear it. Will Sammos protect her if he fails even to protect his own Sacred City?"

Agriabus moaned aloud at these words and the fire before them blazed higher as if voicing the great god's own disapproval. *'Never has the Emperor spoken thus.'* "Sire, you *must* not say these things! With all of the respect that a servant can have for his master, I say this. Faith shall vindicate us. Hope shall sustain us. And love – for Sammos, for the Empire, for *you* – will enable us to endure anything. It can and it must!"

"Aaah," said Callimach, exhaling, and his body, which had become rigid with urgency when he had spoken of his niece, now seemed slowly to shrink once again and to become like that of a wraith once more, "Faith and Hope. But do you have *faith* in the fidelity of your son, Agriabus, and do you *hope* to see his redemption in this life?"

Agriabus tottered and almost fell from the couch to the marble floor. He clutched his face with his hands, suppressing a choke.

"I have heard that the Krahl has become quite fond of the young man Sulcharek and has given him a position at Court and that, further, he has been granted a title and lands in Pentes – when it is all over." Callimach snorted. "A 'Lord of Odrum' he will be. No less."

Agriabus clutched himself so tightly around the chest that he could not breathe, his Purple-lined robes twisted in knots about his body. "How....?" he rasped in a voice so quiet it was barely audible over the hissing flames of the fire. The priest shuffled slowly from one end of the Altar to the other in front of them, flinging the fat into the flames. "How did you come by this knowledge, My Lord?"

The Emperor regarded him a while and Agriabus saw that his gaze was now kind yet sad. "The Novices of Sammos have brought me such news as they have deemed valuable. I still have many eyes and ears in the City – and even a few still beyond its Walls." He sighed, a deep, deep sigh. "Now kiss me, my old friend, and go from here. Go back into the City, back into life, and leave me here. Sammkos cannot do without her Prefect."

A scream threatened to burst from Agriabus's lips: *'Nor can she do without her Lord and Emperor!'* But perhaps it would not make a difference. Perhaps it was too late. With trembling hands, he reached out and grasped the Emperor's limp hand which lay in his lap in the coarse cloth of the Penitent shift. Agriabus lifted it and pressed its cold, thin, dry, parchment skin urgently to his lips. Then, releasing it, he rose with as much grace and dignity as his leg would allow him.

"My Lord, I do take my leave," he intoned gravely, looking down at Callimach, who had returned his eyes to the sacred fire of the Altar, "but faith I have and hope I have. And I not the only one. And love - *that* is had by all who dwell in Sammkos and it is directed toward the one who is ordained by Divine decree as Lord of this City and of this Land."

Agriabus turned and strode toward the Altar before which he knelt, biting down the flaring pain in his right leg, and bowed his head. The Priest came and sprinkled some of the fat upon his head and chanted briefly over him. Agriabus then rose carefully and turned to go.

And his eyes fell upon something partly hidden in the shadows, set against the far wall, and near to the Statue of Sammos. It was the Emperor's armour, helm, shield, and sword. As he beheld the renowned, long-hilted blade, he caught the flicker of the flames upon the tiny ruby eyes of the face of the great god of Sammar set in its pommel.

He turned and walked from the Shrine and a sudden thought came to him. *'I did not ask of him the reason for the votive candles. I did not ask him the nature of his vow.'*

II

Seuton hastened up to him as he stood outside the iron doors. "Does he send word? What are his commands, Lord Prefect?" The soldier's dull red cape swirled behind him and he held his helm under his left arm. His sword was at his side and he was in full black armour.

Agriabus sighed inwardly at the Captain's well-meaning zealousness. *'Does he not know the slender thread upon which the Empire hangs?'* He held up a cautioning hand in the man's very face. "The Emperor conveys his appreciation for your firm vigilance and is earnestly seeking the will of Sammos in high matters of State," said Agriabus, evenly, looking into the soldier's keen, dark eyes, "He is aware of all that is transpiring in and around the City and urges all soldiers of the Empire to discharge their solemn duties to their utmost."

It was dry tripe and the Captain of the Imperial Guard knew it but he lowered his eyes nevertheless, accepting even this tasteless morsel as a repast for his troubled soul. Agriabus looked up. Many other Guards in the outer courtyard of the Shrine were watching and listening to their every word, eyes wide. *'The thread is slender indeed.'*

"Where is the Lord Tistertich?" he asked, loudly.

"He comes even now," answered another guard who looked to be no more than a youth. He stood aside and Agriabus caught sight of the old, one-eyed Lord Engineer of the City hobbling quickly across the stone courtyard, leaning on a tall staff of yew wood.

"My Lord Prefect! Lord Agriabus!" Tistertich bellowed, "You must come. Quickly!"

The Guard parted before the stoop-shouldered, black-robed civic official as pigeons might part before a shrieking child tearing through the centre of Sammar Gloria. As Tistertich approached, Agriabus was startled to see that he shook violently within his robes and that his one eye looked to be aflame with a virulent fever.

Agriabus took an involuntary step backward, for the Red Ague had raged through the Glorious City many times over the last several years and even now was racing through the devastated areas outside the walls of Sammkos. It was said that it followed closely behind the destroying armies of the Krahl, acting like a second blight of devastation upon the Holy Empire.

But the Lord Engineer was now clutching at his robes of Purple and Agriabus forced himself to meet the wild, almost mad gaze of that single, black eye.

"The tunnels!" Tistertich screeched at him, "The Odrum tunnels! We can stop them. We can *stop* them, by Sammos!"

Agriabus was stunned. "Stop them?" he repeated, "But my Lord, have you come here unaccompanied from the Heratikkon? You must have a detail at all times! You are too valuable now to the survival of the Empire. I have given strict orders, in the name of the Emperor, for *all* Ministers - "

But Tistertich was impatiently waving his arm at him. "Never mind that, never mind that!" he barked, hoarsely, "The men are occupied fully in the task of survival as it is and these tidings cannot wait. I have made do with all haste with only my driver and carriage from the Heratikkon Wall, aye, and we are losing time in returning to it as it is. We must go now!"

"Commander!" Agriabus barked at once, turning again to Seuton, "I need you to spare for me two riders as escort for the Lord Tistertich and me in his carriage out of the Inner City and to the Heratikkon."

The two riders-at-arms of the Imperial Guard in their black armour and red capes flanked the carriage as it made its way north from the Shrine of Sammos and through Sammar Gloria, teetering on its pinioned axles and squeaking wheels. Agriabus sat opposite Tistertich within, his robes affording only meagre cushioning against the hard, bare bench. He found, however, that the pain in his leg had dulled to merely a low-key protest. He smiled, tightly. *An improvement, at least.'* He glanced curiously at the Lord Engineer as the carriage groaned and bounced.

Tistertich, leaning eagerly forward, was now staring intently out of the open window of the carriage toward the west, craning his neck and impatiently swivelling his one, good eye - the right - to and fro. Agriabus knew that there was nothing to see here in the great square of the capital except for the huge alabaster statues of Callimach's forebears. They ringed the 'Gloria' in three concentric circles radiating out from the Shrine like glittering white spokes in a vast wheel with the Shrine at its hub. Even Callimach's father's image was here somewhere in their midst. *'And may they stand forever. Each one.'*

"What is it that you wish to show me, Tistertich," said Agriabus, softly, his eyes not leaving the other man's lined, yet taut face.

Tistertich started and turned toward him. His eye was still bright and feverish. "Show you, My Lord Prefect?" he said, unsteadily, "Only the deliverance of Sammar. *That* is what I wish to show you. But we have precious little time. Far less, in fact, than you can possibly imagine."

"The Walls….?"

"….will not last this very day." That black eye bore into his until it became almost hypnotic. "When the sun sinks below the horizon tonight and this day has at last given up its ghost, all who are left alive in this City will wait in vain for the dawn. Unless…." His voice trailed off.

Agriabus felt his chest constrict and he reached up and gripped the ledge of the window. The air seemed sucked out of the carriage and he began to choke again just as he had done shamefully within the Shrine in his Master's presence. *I cannot control myself any longer. Is it all really over?* Convulsively, he clutched at the throat of his Purple robes with his other hand. Tistertich watched him calmly, almost serenely, his one eye now suddenly glistening.

"But Sammkos may yet be saved." It was a whisper, a faint, ghostly breath from the Lord Engineer's lips. "If you believe in miracles."

They passed through the gate between the halls of the Imperial Palace that housed the Ministers and their families and the Guards stationed at its wide doors saluted. Two hundred years before, when the occupation of the City by the Ladrians, Sammar's erstwhile and yet treacherous allies, had finally been ended and Sammkite authority re-established within its great walls, the new line of Emperors – Callimach's own family– had abandoned these halls of the Palace, which encircled the Gloria, and had left them to the City's administrators.

The old, creaking carriage rumbled onto the cobbled Heratikkon Road.

Tistertich abruptly lifted his staff and rapped the ceiling of the carriage sharply with its gnarled haft. "Faster!" he shouted, "It will be near to evening ere we come to it! By Sammos!"

Agriabus heard the driver's shrill, almost panicky reply from atop his box. "But, My Lord, the Road is perilous even at our present speed!"

"PAHH!" snorted Tistertich at that, "Never you mind. Just *fly!*"

"Yes, My Lord." Agriabus heard the snapping of a whip and the snorting and whinnying of the carriage horses and then felt the ponderous vehicle shudder beneath him. The desolate, dusty fields surrounding the Imperial Palace began to move more swiftly past the windows and indeed a cloud of dust was soon drifting through the inside of the carriage. Agriabus sneezed involuntarily and passed a fold of his Purple robes over the lower half of his face. He knew that what the driver had said concerning the condition of the Road was all too true and he deliberately gained a firm handhold on the window ledge and on the edge of the bench beside him. It was going to be rough and he did not like to think about what kind of protest his leg would give him at their journey's end. He glanced once more at the Lord Engineer and now found that the old man was gazing, grimly, clear past him toward the end of the carriage, his teeth grinding together, and his coal-black eye blazing.

They drew near to the meagre, grouped lodgings and dwellings of the citizens of Heratikkon, the northern section of Sammkos. Agriabus leaned forward toward the window and winced. He grasped his right leg with both hands and began to knead his thigh through his robes but it was no good. It was on fire and he was only making it worse. He gritted his teeth. He would have to bear it. Grinding his own teeth, then, he leaned out of the open window.

Outside, stood the houses of the Guilds of Textiles; the Tailors and Weavers and Coopers and Tanners of Sammkos. They were the only ones who lived here now for it was the sparsest and poorest of the four sections of the Glorious City. Even within Agriabus' own lifetime, he could remember when Heratikkon teemed with sellers and warers who did not close their shops until late into the night. He had travelled to Sammkos a few times with his father as a child on long excursions from Pentes, once even by ship across the Golden Lake itself. It had been his father who had taken their own family line out from beneath the shadow of the name 'Outlander' and had enabled he, Agriabus, to obtain education and training unthinkable to that same father. *'Father, I owe you no less than my life. If only I could pass on the knowledge of that gift to my son.'*

The Heratikkon Wall rose up before the carriage and the memories of the past fled from Agriabus' mind. He leaned out as far as he dared in the face of a sudden stabbing pain in his leg and could see its fast-rising bulk looming ahead. Soon, he could make out its individual stones, cracked and ancient and dry as dust in the climbing rays of the sun. He saw their immensity....

....and then, somehow, he saw the hands that built them.

Into his mind, unbidden but with a power so fierce and strong, came vivid images from the Long Past. He saw tools, ramps, ropes. He saw groaning, straining bodies of men, heard wails and moans of dying beasts. He smelt sweat and dung and choking dust. He felt a furnace of relentless, baking sun. He saw the Empire.

He knew and felt the power of its long ago birth and the vitality of its long, full life. And in that knowing and feeling, he perceived its death – inexorable and approaching.

It was not even a thing to be mourned.

No. This also he saw. The Holy Empire of Sammar had lived its life, had left its mark upon the very face of the world. And that was enough. This was its legacy and its privilege in the sight of both men and Divine. Nothing could deny it or erase it. No force, no calamity, no armies – no man.

Yet there were still those, he knew, within Sammkos' faltering Walls who had yet to see and know and accept this truth; this Reckoning.

The crushing weight of the centuries that lay upon the Wall therefore fell upon Agriabus, Prefect of the Purple of Sammkos. In an instant, he was stepping from the carriage without being aware that it had stopped or that he had opened its door, unaware even of the pain in his leg. Staggering and gasping, he lurched toward the ancient stones and laid a trembling hand upon them. In the swift-rising, morning sun, the Wall's growing heat entered into him through his fingertips and he allowed it to fill him up, to banish the cold and the chill of the Shrine. *The life of the City is here and not there. What is left of it. I will not go back to that place before the End. Not even if my Master does not leave it.*

An Imperial Guard was standing at his elbow. "My Lord," he murmured, "are you quite well?"

III

"The Walls," he whispered, "The Walls will fall."

"My Lord?"

Agriabus gave a start and turned to look at the red-caped, black-armoured soldier standing beside him. He blinked. "A dream," he said, quietly, "That is all."

The soldier nodded and then gestured toward the Lord Engineer, who was hobbling quickly toward them, clacking his iron-heeled yew staff briskly before him upon the flags of the Road. "He's just there," cried Tistertich, pointing away east along the foot of the Wall, "Not twenty paces along the Road. Come! The time is nearly upon us."

Iustos de Freganza. Agriabus winced inwardly at the sight of him. The huge Parrian soldier-of-fortune, draped in black cape trimmed with serge and standing well over four cubits in height, greeted him curtly beneath the Wall with the sun peering just over his left shoulder.

The huge mercenary commander had arrived at the City a fortnight past, just before the Odrum had succeeded in closing the Western approach to Sammkos with their Horse, finally sealing its fate, and offering the great-swords of he and his three hundred men to the service of Sammar – such as could still be rendered. And Agriabus had not trusted it. Callimach, however, in light of the dire need of the Empire, had readily and enthusiastically received him and the two, Agriabus knew, had then closeted themselves together for an afternoon, making plans and schemes the knowledge of which he had not been privy. Freganza and his so-called 'Free Knights' were then the next ten days seen organizing and moving themselves throughout the City, the leader's great figure, itself, sometimes being seen formidably stumping upon the very Walls of Sammkos. It was said that the Odrum soldiers all around the City had quickly begun to wager on which of them could skewer the man with a crossbow bolt attached to a rope and haul his carcass off the Wall to present as a gift to the Krahl. Agriabus did not doubt the story. For the past two days, however, he had had it from many sources – for he too had informants around the City – that the mercenary had been meeting with the Lord Engineer alone, not showing his face, even to eat.

The small-folk who had taken refuge within the City and who knew anything about the matter had, of course, assumed the worst - that the two men, the one over-reckless and the other too clever by half, despairing of any deliverance by Sammos, had resorted to seeking the City's salvation through horrific rites of pagan Scalan ritual and Dark Magic.

Agriabus, standing now in the strange, dark man's very shadow, shuddered within his Purple robes. *And who is to say they are wrong?* Freganza's gauntlets, he noted, were grasped in one of the man's, ham-sized fists. Evidently he had just been intently watching over his soldiers as they laboured at unguessed tasks before the foot of the Wall and was loath to interrupt his scowling vigil.

"My Lords," rumbled the big man, taking in both he and Tistertich with a sweep of his slate-grey eyes, "the preparations are complete and we are now only awaiting the breakthrough." He eyed Agriabus, pointedly. "I daresay you'll be able to report something that will finally energize that Purple Master of yours, Lord Prefect. If you'll follow me….."

Agriabus tensed at this bald shot at the Emperor and ground his teeth together as the big man then turned on his heels and led them - a huge, dark, grim spectre - farther along the cobbled road beside the Wall. Tistertich urgently grasped his arm and coaxed him forward. With a sudden flare-up, he felt the agony in his leg once more and could scarcely keep his feet. "Wait and see, My Lord Prefect," the tottering, old Engineer grated in his ear, "Wait and see now the glorious deliverance of Sammkos."

Glorious…..or cursed?

A peculiar smell thrust itself, powerfully, into his nostrils. He gagged and drew an arm before his face. *Sweet and sickly-sour at once. What is this foul odour?* It was a strange mixture of more than one scent but he could not place them. Holding his nose, he drew up cautiously to where Freganza's knights were assembled. He saw at once that they were crowded around an enormous hole in the ground. *By Sammos!* Some were grasping and leaning over great, black vats which stood at the very lip of the maw and others held pails in their hands. Behind them all, Agriabus caught sight of still others standing by with spades in hand. *What in the Name of Sammos is all this capery?*

Tistertich was squinting at him through his one, still-shining, feverish, black eye. "You detect the presence of sulfur," whispered the Lord Engineer, "do you not?"

"Is that what this foul stench is? But surely something else…..?"

"Aye, it is mixed with something more: Naphtha."

"Naphtha!" Agriabus jerked his head away from the hole and toward Tistertich and before them, Freganza turned to peer briefly over his shoulder at them. Agriabus felt his flesh crawl. "Not since the ancient Guild was disbanded, Tistertich," he hissed at the other man, "has that foul substance been handled. It is said that it can burn on contact. It is black witchery!"

Freganza laughed and came to a halt, turning around to face them. He crossed his massive arms over his chest and watched them, a derisive sneer twisted on his lips.

"It is a natural substance known to the Ancients - " sputtered Tistertich ("Scalans," muttered Agriabus) " – known to the Ancients to have certain…..incendiary properties when mixed with other elements. Nothing more."

Freganza held up his arm. "Oh, quiet now, you frightened maidens! They're near."

Agriabus's retort died on his lips. Below them, *beneath* them, he heard now quite plainly a scraping and shuffling sound. It was coming from the depths of the pit itself.

Like demons from hell. It is the Odrum army ascending to destroy us all!

"Wait," murmured Freganza to his men through thin lips, arm still upraised, "Not too soon. Let them come first.....Let them come."

Let them come? My great, dread Sammos, are we gathered here to be slaughtered?

He was about to snatch his blade from his scabbard at his side, about to fight and die for Empire and Master, when suddenly the huge Parrian made a vicious down-cut with his arm, even as the first cries of the enemy burst forth from the pit.

The assembled knights upturned their strange, black pots into the hole, those with pails flung their contents after.

And he barely registered the freakish light, the queer, snaking fire, and the sudden, blazing, hellish heat. The screams in the midst of it all were like nothing human, transforming themselves in an instant from cries and shouts of battle-lust to shrieks of unimaginable agony. A grisly inferno engulfed them all.

Goose-prickles standing out all over his flesh, he flung himself backward from the damned, black pit and its writhing carnage within it, the stench now so overpowering that his eyes streamed and he fell to his knees and retched on the flags of the Road over and over again.

"That's it!" he heard the great voice of Freganza bellowing above the tumult. "Send them back to the wombs of their *bitches* of mothers!"

Then Tistertich was there, pulling on his arm once more. The pain shooting up from his leg was unbearable and he staggered mightily before he could even turn to look the other man in the face.

"It was the only way," the old man was babbling in his ear, "the only way to stop them. Don't you see? The only way to save the City."

IV

They were all there, waiting. In the charged silence, he could sense the barely-suppressed emotions surging through all of the tense bodies around him. It was two hours past sunrise. *We should be out there now ending it. I should be out there ending* him. His hand convulsed on the hilt of his sword. He gritted his teeth. *Where is he?*

Keeping his sword firmly sheathed but its hilt in a death-grip, he darted his eyes to the faces of the other men in the pavilion, especially those standing to either side of the centre table. Adjeek, Commander of the Seljen, the Master's elite Guard, and Tris el-Dafek, Master of Men, stood in the places of honour; to the right and to the left of *his* chair. *Or would so if he ever showed himself.* These men, he knew, were the two finest warriors in the Centre Land and respected as such. They were also ever scheming against each other and it was said that the Master encouraged this rivalry for it served his purposes in keeping all beneath him disunited in their own ambitions and beholden to him. Raenis ad-Dura, the Whisperer, was half-hidden within the folds of his high, black cloak utterly motionless and silent beside the Guard Commander and Edro of Sarragoze, Master of Horse, stood next to el-Dafek, his fearsome scimitar girt at his side and an ever-present scowl twisting his leathern face. Next to ad-Dura, in the third rank from the Master, loomed Belgen Ghour, the Faloud, with his massive battle-axe strapped to his back.

Where Adjeek, the Guard Commander, stood for unquestioned honour, *this* man, Sulcharek had quickly come to appreciate, stood for all that the Master required to be done that was perhaps a little *less* honourable.

He allowed his surreptitious gaze to linger longest upon the scarred, stoic face of the renowned 'Outlander.' He knew that Ghour's distant, seething, turbulent land east of Odrum had, in the last generation of fathers, been vanquished once and for all by the Krahl's great armies but that the tall warrior himself had come to the attention of the Master for his secret and lethal deeds. He was now in such favour that his voice, as they had it here, was 'ever near to the Master's ear.' This, he, Sulcharek, set store by. He would be for Sammar even as Ghour was and remained for distant, lost, defeated Faloud. Would he not? He also would add lustre to the epithet 'Outlander.' For, once his deluded, anachronistic father and his beaten master were at last gone the way of the great, ancient beasts of the Dawn Age, once those old, crumbling walls outside this very tent were no more than heaps of rubble, he and he alone, would represent the Name of Sammar to the posterity of men. And this steeled the heart of Sulcharek of Pentes. For this, he would gladly be all that the Master required him to be.

And right now that was patient.

He growled deep within his throat. *Everything is ready. EVERYTHING.* His eyes fell upon the broad, faded, creased map of Sammkos that lay upon the table. It was old, he saw, yet still served. *The walls, the tunnels, the gates, the men, even the Signs, all are in place. Yet he delays. It is -*

There was a stirring of the canvas behind the head of the table.

He looked up in time to see Tufek, the Mouse, steal into the great tent. The boy's tiny, gold-trimmed cap was tilted back on his head, almost lost within his long, dark, tousled hair.

"Harken now, Lords!" cried the scrawny urchin, raising his thin arms and shaking them beseechingly, "Harken now to my Master and he will harken to you." He scampered forward and grasped the worn, simple folding-chair that stood before the head of the table and the great men who stood there. He drew it back slightly and leaned his elbows upon its high, canvas back. "Yes, that he will. For he is true, my Master is." He gazed round at each of them placidly, his chin propped in his hands.

"True," agreed the Guard Commander in a rich, bass rumble and Sulcharek heard a scattering of assenting noises within the tent. "Yes, Noble Adjeek," said the Mouse, turning toward him and accosting him with a raised, grimy finger, "you have the *truth* of it." Absurdly, the Commander smiled as if pleased with himself.

This is getting us nowhere.

"He approaches now," shouted Tufek then and abruptly standing stiff and attentive beside his Master's chair. At once, every man in the pavilion, Sulcharek included, became as rigid as stone. "He approaches and harkens, himself, giving due honour unto the Spirit of the World!" The boy looked round at them again, this time with bright, wide eyes. "Who gives due unto the Spirit of the World?" he shouted.

"Krahl!" thundered the men within the great tent and Sulcharek joined his voice to theirs.

The Master entered, wordlessly, and seated himself in the unadorned chair.

All eyes were upon him. Stunned, Sulcharek realized that he wore his loose, satin court robes. *No garbs of war these.* His heart sank within him. *He is not ready.* The silence in the tent was utter. A deep frown was etched on the Master's lined face, as plain as the plight of their enemy beyond the canvas walls. Indeed, his hardened visage reminded Sulcharek of the fractures within an open space of flat, parched ground that hadn't seen water in an age. His black eyes, which had burned with a martial fervour when Sulcharek had first been ushered into his presence upon leaving the City almost twenty days past, were now lit by something else, something which he, Sulcharek, could not fathom. *Rage, perhaps, yet not a wholesome, urging one that guides to victory but a corrosive, gnawing one that eats away at the inside.*

He watched as his new Master slowly cast his dark gaze around at them. Then the black eyes shut tight. "Tonic!" the man thundered.

The Mouse was already moving, scampering to retrieve a steaming horn from a slave at the door. He brought it back to his Master and Sulcharek watched as the Krahl snatched it out of his hand and held it to his lips, downing it in one gulp. "AH!" the man rumbled, wiping his mouth with the sleeve of his robe. With a slight twinge of disgust, Sulcharek saw that some of the dark liquid had dribbled into the Krahl's black, tangled beard, and even down onto the table where it made drops the colour of dark blood. *It is the draught of his crack-pot doctor.* He gave a start. *Ah, I see it now. His right hand is gnarled. It clutches at the vessel with such unnatural desperation. It is his arthritis.*

The Krahl carefully set the empty horn down beside him. "That is enough for now, my little Mouse," he said, nodding at the scrawny child, and the boy bowed and scampered from the tent. Irritably, the Krahl then motioned to the men at the table. "Sit!" he commanded. They sat. Sulcharek had to resist an urge to move forward as they did so for he knew that only the great men sat. He must to wait to be invited, personally, by the Master in order that he might then advance before the eyes of all and join them on an equal footing. This he had counseled himself to do from past observations. And thus was he convinced of his own inevitable rise. *Yes. When the time is right.*

"Adjeek," said the Master, his voice a dry rasp.

"Master," said the Commander, "may the World Spirit be honoured today." He pointed to the map spread out before them. "We stand ready at the Western Gate of Sammkos this very minute to lead the onslaught against our enemies. Their defenses are smoke, their walls webs. The Guard is hungry and awaits only your command. The enemy is surely delivered to us."

A slight scowl showed on the Krahl's face at this glittering appraisal of which Sulcharek had managed to catch most in his rudimentary Odrum. He saw the Master then nod toward the other side of the table. "Dafek."

"Show me a Sammkite head – or a Sammkite teat for that matter - and the boys will cut it off, Master."

"Huh," grunted the Krahl, "I see your snappy tongue is ready, at the least. I confess I do much prefer a severed Sammkite head to an attached one." His black eyes roved through the tent as if seeking one. *Or a certain one.* Sulcharek gave an uncomfortable shudder. Again, he had managed to get the drift of the words. The men at the table laughed uneasily for the strangely grim mood had not been lifted. Sulcharek found himself the only one in the tent who did not join in except for the big Faloud. He noticed that Belgen Ghour's stoic gaze never left the Krahl. "And how fares the Fire-Tube? Is it emplaced?"

"Aye, Master," said Dafek, "It has been brought through the forest by courageous means and set atop the First Hill as planned." He glanced toward Edro seated beside him. "The Horse have assisted the Men in this great endeavour."

Again the Master grunted. "And I know what you have for me, Dura," he growled, turning to the Whisperer. He lifted both, scarred arms into the air. "The decree of the Heavens."

"Master," murmured ad-Dura, leaning forward over the table so that his elbows all but blotted out the West Gate of Sammkos from the map, "the dimming of the Moon last night by the shadow of the World did indeed signal the pleasure and timing of the Spirit. Of this did I make certain to appraise you. Such high duties do you entrust to me and yet I have other duties to which you have bid me attend. With my Master's permission I shall enlighten him of a further matter."

The Krahl, scowl still in place, jerked his arm out before him in a curt invitation and leaned back in his austere chair. Sulcharek watched as the black-clad spymaster then rose and called to the guards at the far opening of the pavilion. "Let him come!"

There was a stirring and a man entered the tent as if thrust into it from behind. Stumbling slightly, he looked up and around and then, seeing the Krahl, began to step tentatively towards him.

"Hah!" said the Krahl, "More Sammkites!"

Again there was a nervous laughter and with another start, Sulcharek recognized the newcomer. *Lantass! I might have known that he was playing both sides of the coin.* He watched as the Sammkite spymaster, now slightly stooped and greying at the temples, rigidly approached the table. "Master," he said tightly, and in earnest Odrum, "I have witnessed, even this morning, a spectacle within the City so Barbaric that the Emperor's noble dynasty is thrice-damned even before it falls." The Krahl, the scowl disappearing from his face, sat up attentively in his camp-chair at this, dark eyes fixed upon the speaker. "He has, with the odious assistance of Iustos de Freganza - the barbaric Parrian with whom I know more than one man in this place is acquainted - resurrected the secrets of the Scalan Alchemists and has unleashed the Fiends-Fire upon your noble soldiers beneath the Heratikkon Wall."

An outcry of consternation and rage arose at this. Sulcharek added his own voice to the tumult. *The mad, old fool! Does he not fear the Divine? I knew he was desperate but this - ?* The Krahl shot a gnarled fist - his left - into the air and the clamour subsided.

"What did it do," the Master rasped, "this Fiends-Fire? For I have heard of it in tales spoken to me long ago by my Sammkite nurse. Fantasies, I call them."

Lantass swallowed. "Not fantasies, Master. There do exist flames in this world so unholy that men do not set them. Leastways not sane men. I saw flesh slough from bone like wax sloughing from a candle and then bones begin to char to ash before my very eyes. I did not see the rest as I hastened here but surely nothing is left within that pit beneath that wall where once had been men."

The black eyes glimmered. "No," the Krahl grated. His fist, still clutched and raised in the air, trembled. "Not what it did to my noble soldiers. What did it do to the tunnel? The tunnel. Can it still be used?"

Sulcharek caught the high officers and great warriors glance at one another uncertainly.

" 'Used', Master?" said Lantass, perplexed.

"Yes," said the Krahl, his voice now little more than a croak, "can it still be traversed either from within or from without?"

Lantass slowly shook his head. "With that fire it is sure that…..the tunnel…..is sealed. Cauterized."

"Ah!" The Krahl sat back heavily in his chair once more. "'Cauterized,'" he murmured, eyes unfocussed and gazing afar, "Like closing a gashed wound with a glowing blade."

The Sammkite spymaster trembled. "Very like, Master," he whispered, "but where one way is shut another opens."

The Krahl re-focused on him and Sulcharek saw the scowl once more appear on the hardened features. "Explain," he growled.

"Master," interjected ad-Dura, "it has come to my attention just as this venerable council was convening - by my Sammkite counterpart here -" he nodded at Lantass – "that the City of Sammkos is already opened to us."

There was a slight stirring in the tent. Sulcharek took in a breath.

"Hmm," rumbled the Krahl, the scowl deepening in his lined face.

"Master," resumed Lantass, meaningfully, "the Dalcos Wall in the Mestian Quarter is breached. I have seen it myself. The opening is well hidden but not insignificant."

"And it is no longer watched with the same vigilance as the other three." Ad-Dura extended a single, pale finger into the air. "For it faces the Lake and the ships of the fleet there have purposely laid off by your recent command."

Sulcharek saw the scowl flicker for the briefest of moments upon the Krahl's dark face. *We have him now.* His grip upon the hilt of his sword tightened anew. Then, slowly, the Krahl leant back in his chair, his hands steepled before his face. A deep hush fell once more.

When the Krahl slammed his fist onto the table - again, his good one, the left – everyone, Sulcharek included, jumped. The map slithered to the ground between Adjeek and ad-Dura with a quiet rustle.

The Master rose to his feet. "The Command is ready!" he cried, "The Fire-Tube is in place! The Men are poised to strike heads from shoulders!" He glared around at all of them and they, mystified, returned his look in stunned silence. He thrust his gnarled fist in the air. "The *Moon* is swallowed up by the shadow of the World!" Again a pause. Sulcharek, with a gulp, quickly looked round at the other men. Those sitting at the table sat utterly still, eyes straight ahead. A few standing around the table swayed where they stood, uncertain.

What is all this? We know it is time!

"Walls are breached," the Krahl thundered, sweeping both his hands down toward the ground. Another pause. He began to pace, slowly and deliberately, around the table, his hands behind his back, and the men who stood, bewildered, began to stumble out of his way. Sulcharek, utterly lost, stepped back as well. He watched as the Krahl paused behind ad-Dura and grasped the back of his chair as best he could with both hands. "Hmm?" said the Master, peering down at the back of ad-Dura's head. The spymaster did not answer but Sulcharek saw the web-weaver seem to shrink even farther down within his high collar.

"The battle is *won!*" shouted the Krahl, finally, to the whole pavilion, raising his arms to the heavens.

But none shouted out as if it were a victory cry. Only a dead silence followed.

Lowering his arms, the Krahl slowly continued around the table in that deep quiet, passing within an arm's length of Sulcharek of Pentes. Then, whirling, the Odrum Master looked him dead in the face and the Sammkite lordling gasped.

"But where is *he?*" whispered the Krahl. "Where is Callimach XI of Sammar?"

"Master," murmured ad-Dura, after several moments' awkward silence. "You know where he is; where he has been these last several - "

Impatiently, the Krahl sliced a hand through the air and the spymaster clamped his mouth shut. Striding purposefully back to his chair, the Krahl faced them once more and swept his lingering dark gaze around the tent. "Let me tell you, O Great Men of Odrum," he said, almost serenely now, "how wars are fought." Sulcharek stared hard at him, heart hammering, trying to catch every word. "They are not fought by soldiers or officers; not by horses or weapons or breaches. They are not fought by cosmic cycles or engineering accidents. No." His steely, black eyes flashed and he extended a single finger – this one straight and true – into the air. "They are fought by gods and kings. *Gods and kings!*"

This last was a scream so loud that Sulcharek flinched and he caught spittle flying from the Master's lips.

A silence so utter followed this that Sulcharek could hear his heart pounding in his ears and in his head. Stirring uncomfortably, he beheld the Krahl's raised finger slowly lower itself and point, trembling, toward the side of the pavilion.

"This," sputtered the Krahl, "is not War. It is a capitulation. A shameful insult to all gods and kings who have ever gone to war." He lowered his arm to his side. "You all say you are ready for your glorious battle. Very well. Go. Have your slaughter. I will have none of it."

"Master -," began Adjeek, shakily, eyes widening, "where will you be if not - "

"I will be at the Second Hill," cut in the Krahl, acidly, turning on him, "as planned in the event of an.….unforeseen catastrophe." His wide lips twisted sardonically. "From there I will be watching this farce unfold with my glass until *he* should deign to appear and not *cheat* me of my proper glory. Is that clear enough for you?"

"But Master," the Guard Commander blurted, "You.….the Command.….They must never be apart. *I* must never be apart from you.….."

A sinister, yet gleeful smile invaded the Krahl's dark face which Sulcharek saw did not touch his black eyes. "Then I guess you and my glorious Seljen will have to stand down, Commander. Is *that* clear enough for you?"

Adjeek, stunned and ashen-faced, slumped in his chair.

"Dafek. Edro," snapped the Krahl, raising his black eyes to them. Both men stiffened in their own chairs. "Fire the Tube when you will. Get this over with." He swept his angry gaze around at the rest of them. "Now get out."

Every man hastened to rise or to turn to go, Sulcharek included, when he heard the Master call out, "Except you." He turned to find the finger pointed once more, this time at his very face. It then swept across to Belgen Ghour, who was only now just rising to his feet. "And you, my fine Faloud. I have something very special in mind for the both of you. And you must make haste."

V

"Tistertich," said Agriabus, head still reeling, "there has been a second assault upon the Sacred Empire."

"My Lord," said the old Engineer, "of what do you speak?" His one eye narrowed. "Are you unwell?"

"Oh, do not mind me!" said Agriabus, testily, "It is Sammar that we must concern ourselves with now, isn't it? And now that you have gone and done this accursed thing, it cannot be *un*done." He wiped his forehead with the back of a shaking hand. *"This* is the second assault." He gestured toward the Wall with its new, slurried pit beneath it with both hands. "This Fiends-Fire direct from the Pagan Scala. Is it not enough that the barbarian Scoffer is already poised to break into this sacred City and defile it? Must you do so before ever he sets foot in it? Now you have done more to shame it than he could possibly do – or even my traitorous *son!"*

Tistertich gaped at him. "Lord Prefect," he spluttered, "do you possibly compare *me* with-"

"Sammos knows that we are desperate," cut in Agriabus, angrily, "and I pray that he will forgive us for this blasphemous sorcery. But now we must hasten to the places where the dignity of our offices require us to be. For the End comes very swiftly now, Sir. I can feel it. And when it comes, we must meet it honourably." He scowled at the other imperial officer. "And not like this." He jerked his head toward the pit.

The single, black eye fastened on him, spitefully. "And not dishonourably, you mean. Is that what you are saying, Lord Prefect? I resent that charge." With a thrust of his staff, the Engineer also indicated the Wall. "Do you not see that it is Sammos Himself who has given us this last chance to stop the Odrum? *Sammos himself* - for it is no less than a miracle!"

"Where is Freganza?" Agriabus shouted over him.

"Freganza and some of his knights are carrying what is left of the substance to the Southern Wall. *There* we will stop up that tunnel as well! Don't you see? There was so precious little of it that could be manufactured - "

"Soldier!" Agriabus yelled, whirling toward one of the imperial guards who had accompanied them to the Wall. He had to bite down on a scream of pain for his leg was now burning as if it were itself doused in Fiends-Fire.

One of the Guards hastened up to him. "My Lord?" he asked.

Agriabus gritted his teeth and gasped, "Take your partner and gather such numbers of your fellows as you can muster in this Quarter and then proceed with all haste to the Southern Wall." He took in a ragged breath. "There you will arrest Iustos de Freganza in the name of the Emperor."

"My Lord?" stammered the soldier, ashen-faced.

"You heard me, soldier," Agriabus growled. "Now go! The time is almost gone."

Swallowing audibly, eyes wide, the young man murmured, "Yes, My Lord."

Agriabus, grim and despairing, watched him turn and hastily depart.

"Lord Prefect," said Tistertich, firmly, "this is a grave error. You have no right. The Emperor himself has given us sanction to do whatever is necessary to save the City. You know this."

Agriabus turned and glared at him. And the words came tumbling out before he could stop them:

"I speak for the Emperor now, Lord Engineer. Is that clear? He is not here. He - " but his throat constricted against the words that had risen like bile to his lips. ' - *has given up,*' they whispered in his head, not to be silenced, *'He has abandoned us all.'*

Staggering on his feet, conscious of the crushing weight upon his heart, Agriabus turned and tilted his head back, looking up once more upon the ancient stones of the Wall. *I cannot revive the mighty glory and honour that once dwelt in this land and covered these Walls. Sammos forgive me, I cannot do it. If either still exist anywhere in this land other than in the storied Past I must find them here and now.....or not at all.*

And never again.

It was at that moment, that the massive Odrum Fire-Tube, crouched upon the hill sixty stadia away, spat its enormous iron shot at the City's West Wall.

And blew half of it to pieces.

Agriabus of Pentes felt the ground shake beneath his feet and heard a sound like thunder roll across the sky above him. *Great Sammos, this is it!*

"Lord Engineer," he heard himself call to Tistertich, his voice echoing in his head, "do not resist and you will be treated leniently. For your name is known even to him."

Dimly, he was aware of the stoop-shouldered engineer's incredulous stare. Head swimming, he turned and drew his sword. Everything slowed, becoming as if a sudden dream, a flight of imagination gone mad. He was vaguely aware that the pain in his leg had even dulled to a distant throb.

Where am I? Am I still within Heratikkon or do I yet rest upon my bed and it is not yet the dawn? Perhaps all that has passed before now has been Dream and I will yet awaken to the real Day and find I must hasten to see him within the Shrine. And persuade him this time to go out and prepare the City.

Now a distant sound like a fierce wind was rising around him, rushing down the road before the Wall. Head reeling now, he glanced quickly at the sky and then at the road toward the west. *No clouds. No dust. What is it?* And then he knew. He began rushing toward the din when suddenly he stopped, frowning, and turned around.….

The rushing wind was from the east, not the west! It was the cry of a horde of Odrum soldiers surging from the direction of the Golden Lake.

But it is not possible! How have they broken through the Dalcos?
There was no time to puzzle it out for the barbarian tide was already lapping around him. At its head was a monstrous man, scarred. Agriabus gaped at him, eyes darting to the immense battle-axe grasped in his huge hands. Then, unthinking and seized by a sudden vehemence, he screamed, "Callimach!" and lunged toward the spectre, sword raised.

The fearsome warrior, not seeing him, turned only in time and Agriabus' blade shivered frightfully against the enormous axe as it shot up with frightening speed to block his wild cut. Charged through with adrenaline and engulfed by a white-hot rage, Agriabus began to rain down blows upon his opponent and the Odrumite had to hasten to interpose his huge weapon between himself and each one. He was vaguely aware that a part of the Odrum throng had hung back to watch the duel and his adversary had to shout at them in an ugly, guttural tongue to get them to move off. All but one did so and yet Agriabus had no time for them. His entire world had shrunk to his opponent and his sword.

And his sword arm was all his body.

Never before had he ever felt such anger. Never before had he ever sensed his blade move with more purpose.

And yet it was not righteous and pure, this anger that had seized him and blazed within him, for even as the huge Odrumite seemed to labour with the strain of his blows, Agriabus felt the transcendent, ineffable rage begin to ebb, sapping him of its exquisite strength. He knew then that it was not given life by some incorruptible and pure conviction of right and truth but rather by a bitter outrage of hurt and fear and betrayal.

And even as his blade faltered with the realization, the huge axe, a sudden blur, got inside his reach.

Catching him broadside against the head – for he had taken no helm with him to the Wall – the blow sent him sprawling in the dust. He rolled insensibly on the ground and, dazed, found himself looking up at the Wall, looming and dancing above him. His leg flared again, a white-hot agony. Dust was in his mouth and he spat, dryly.

Suddenly, a panic seized him. *The pit! I've fallen straight into the Pit to Hell! Sammos have mercy!*

He struggled to rise but his adversary loomed over him, the great axe gripped in his hand. Agriabus fought to bring his blade up but the man merely pushed him back into the dust with the haft of his weapon. Spitting some harsh words at him, he then turned and disappeared.

Agriabus, stunned and blanketed from head to toe in choking dust, coughed. It was to the south that the Odrum brute had departed. It was the same direction as the rest of them. *Toward the Gloria. Toward him.*

"No," he croaked, his throat a parched well. Again, he struggled to rise.

There came a laugh.

At first it was so out of place, so incongruous that Agriabus, staggering to his feet once more, could not register it. After a pause, he jerked his head toward the sound.

The lone Odrum soldier who had not departed with the others stood nearby, almost lazily, leaning on the hilt of his sword. Its blade was stuck into the ground and the Heratikkon Wall with its new pit beneath its feet was just behind him.

"Do you know what he called you just now?" the man said, a ghost of a smile playing on his youthful face. "Purple Man." He pointed at Agriabus. "Only now I think Dirty Man might be more in order, don't you?"

Agriabus, frowning, squinted down at his caked robe and then back up at the soldier, struggling to absorb what was going on. "What?" he mumbled.

"Not for me, Purple Man," said the stranger. "That's what he said to you just now.....when you were down in the dirt. Just like the last time I saw you." He took a few steps closer and Agriabus again focused on his face.

The smile widened. "Hello, Father," said the man.

Agriabus answered mechanically, "I have no son."

Sulcahrek tilted his head. "Forgotten so soon, is he? That's a shame. There's still so much that he wants you to remember him by." Casually he lifted his sword.

"What other memory," answered Agriabus, his voice still no more than a croak, "could he possibly want to instill than the one he's already provided; how he abandoned his sworn liege and the land of his birth and ran, tail between his legs, to a cruel master who will have no more use for him when all this is over than a lord has for a cur?"

A shadow flitted across Sulcharek's face and Agriabus had the pleasure of seeing the brazen smirk slide off of it. The younger man took a menacing step towards him but then stopped. The smirk returned and grew more brazen.

"Ah, very good, Father. Baiting me. Trying to get me to do something stupid." He nodded. "Perhaps you *have* learned something since last I saw you."

"I don't have to bait you to do anything stupid," answered Agriabus, lifting his own sword. "You do that quite well on your own. And what I *have* learned since last you saw me is that duty and honour, so utterly incomprehensible to some, still mean something in this world."

Sulcharek laughed, harshly. "Like to His Exalted Imperialness, Callimach XI of Sammar? Or is it only *your* world that we're talking about? A world that's very old and very sad and very small. And very over." He waved at Agriabus with his free hand. "Wake up, Father! There's a new world now. And it's under a new Master."

The rage bubbled and surged within him again. He could feel it. And as much as he knew deep down that it could only count against him, he let it wash over him and take him over completely.

Once more, Agriabus found himself plunging recklessly at his opponent. "I serve Callimach XI of Sammar!" he screamed, swinging his blade. Once more it crashed together with another, this time sending a spark upwards in the air. Once more, he felt the crushing weight of anguish squeeze his heart.

It must be me! It must be me now! I must defend the Empire!

Sulcharek wavered only a moment before recovering and counter-attacking viciously with a sharp cut. This time it was Agriabus, just parrying the move, who wobbled on his feet. Yet, in truth, it was more than that, for one of them, the left, slipped on a stone and he fell hard to the ground on the seat of his breeches, his robe tangled about him.

"Get up, Old Man!" screeched his son. Only it was not his son. It was a spectre whose face was hidden by a shadow, evil, malignant.

He wants to kill me. For true. Agriabus, his leg once more a stabbing agony, somehow, and for the last time, lurched to his feet and faced his son, the son whom he could not acknowledge. Quickly, he doffed his gnarled, smeared robe with its imperial Purple and let it fall to the ground.

Then his anger, so fickle, so volatile, began to slip away again.

By Sammos, I have nothing left. Forgive me. The tip of his sword lowered.

"It is not wise to lower your defences, Father," growled Sulcharek. And quick as a wild cat, he charged in and made another cut with his blade. There was no way that Agriabus could prevent the edge of that blade from reaching its destination.

Shrieking in agony, he crumpled to the ground, holding his right leg. Slowly, thoughts coalesced in his be-numbed brain: *My leg! My leg and my death.*

And then, from far, far away, something else entered into his hazed mind; a sound. The sound of…..

"My Liege," he whispered.

VI

"Sire," said Adjeek, the glass to his right eye, "there is too much dust….."

"Give it here," said the Krahl. "Come on!" He gestured vigorously with his left hand. Both stood beside their mounts atop the Second Hill, below and within the very shadow of the First. They had each covered their ears with their arms at the moment of the Fire-Tube's detonation.

Adjeek passed over the glass at once. The Krahl snatched it from his hand.

"I know that sound," growled the Master, raising the glass to his eye and panning it through the fallen stones of the West Wall of Sammkos. His gaze alighted through the billowing clouds of dust on the milling, surging figures of his noble soldiers as they grappled with the sparse and disjointed Sammkite defenders. "Is it *you?*" he whispered.

"My Master?"

"Sssssst!" He cut off Adjeek with a slash of his hand. "Where are you?" It was a soft murmur. There was a flash of red in the glass.

"Ah!" sighed the Krahl, sharpening his gaze through the still-cloying dust, "Yes. It is a Guard, O Most Noble Adjeek. An Imperial Guard."

Adjeek jerked his head toward his Master. "An *escort?*" he gasped.

The Krahl began to laugh, hoarsely. "My father warned me of his tricks. He's trying to out-fox me, the old Schemer." Abruptly, he thrust the glass back at Adjeek. "If it's true," he growled, "but I fear it is only a ruse."

Hesitantly, Adjeek re-took the glass and held it up to his eye once more. The Krahl scowled down over the clearing of the hill toward the broken city.

"There!" said Adjeek, abruptly, "Yes, I see three, four, maybe five Sammkite soldiers wearing the black armour and the dark red capes. And *there*, just jumping from his mount….."

Snarling, the Krahl seized the glass again from Adjeek's very face and rammed it against his eye.

And then he was there, within his sights.

"Callimach!" he raged. *"Callimach!"*

Within the glass, the Emperor of Sammar was slipping the pin that held his Purple robes and flinging both it and them into the dust. He was holding his great-sword in his right hand and, with the other, was reaching to clutch at the circlet that rested on his brow. This too he cast in the dirt, as if deriding it, scorning its sanctity.

"Ah," said the Krahl, softly, watching, "and now you fight as only a man, do you? How noble."

The black and red Imperial Guards began to surround the austere figure within the narrow confines of the glass, backs to him, capes flapping and marred with dirt, their blades slashing and striking and cutting at the noble Odrum soldiers as they tried to reach him.

The Krahl's mouth twitched.

Then a cry reached his ears through the distant clamour of the battle: *Callimach! Callimach! Behold! Behold!*

He ground his teeth.

"Master?" said Adjeek.

The figure vanished from the glass for a moment and the Krahl panned it urgently once more. "There!" he grunted. His noble soldiers were surging about the doomed, shrinking circle of black and red, hacking it to ribbons, overwhelming it by sheer numbers.

One by one, the Imperial Guards were cut down until only *he* remained, he with his great-sword flashing savage arcs through the dusty air, he wearing nothing but his meagre, coarse shift.

Then he was gone.

With trembling fingers, the Krahl lowered the glass from his face.

"Master," said Adjeek, wide-eyed, "What was it? What did you see?"

"A king," he whispered.

VII

Agriabus, gasping with the pain, peered up at his son, the Wall overshadowing them both. *The Wall of Greatness, the Wall of Glory, the Wall of the long dead Past.* Sulcharek looked, blackly, down at him.

"Now.....you understand," gasped the Lord Prefect of Sammar through clenched teeth. His leg was a raging fire and he fought to keep himself from passing out. *Not until he sees, until he understands. Then he can have me. Then YOU can have me, Great Sammos.*

"You heard it with your own ears, just as I," he grated. "He came. And now the outcome of this selfish, un-holy war does not even matter. For he has won a thousand wars."

"No!" shouted Sulcharek, "No, Old Man! My Master, the Krahl of Odrum, has won it! I have won it!"

Somehow, Agriabus's bloodless lips formed a quivering smile. "You must do now what you have chosen," he whispered, "but as for me, I am a soldier of Sammar." His eyes fluttered briefly before re-focussing upon the man standing over him. "And now.....I follow her and *him*..... into glory.....What do you follow?"

Shrieking with rage, Sulcharek lifted his sword and slashed it downward with all his might.

EPILOGUE

"This is it? You are sure?"

"Yes, Master," rumbled Dafek, "This is what the touman-leader reports. I, myself, did not see it occur but others confirm it."

"You were preoccupied with securing and protecting the body, noticing no other illicit activities."

"No, Master."

Grunting, the Krahl dismounted onto the marble courtyard and the high officers did likewise. He gazed around at the arrayed, alabaster figures. "Sammar Gloria," he said, quietly.

Adjeek stepped close, his face an exaltation of worship. "Master, allow me to assign the Command the task of toppling each statue, smashing it, and hauling it to the cliff of the Mare Nubium. There each and every one of them can be - "

"Are we Barbarians?" cut in the Krahl, sharply, turning on him. Adjeek gaped and lowered his head. "Dafek!" snapped the Master, "Where is this touman-leader?"

Dafek turned and clapped his hands. "Udlass!"

The man came, stout and thick-limbed. Seeing the Master, he flung himself on his knees on the marble stone before him.

The Krahl stared down at him, coldly. "The truth now," he growled, "everything, or by the World Spirit, *you* will be toppled, smashed, and hauled off. Come on!"

"Master," blurted Udlass, "it happened *fast*. There was.....there was....." He darted his eyes to the shrouded litters that lay behind the officers, guarded by a squad of soldiers.

The Krahl briefly turned to look at them before re-focussing upon the man. "There was *him,* lying in the midst of your soldiers. You did not know what to do. Go on."

"It was the Mumblers, Master. The Purple Mumblers."

Frowning, the Krahl turned to Dafek. " 'Mumblers', what is this?"

"Master, they were Priests," said the Master of Men, with a rough clearing of this throat. "Chanting in that ancient gibberish. We did not see them approach. We had not seen them at all. We did not know where they came from." He shrugged his wide shoulders. "Maybe from the dust. But they came after he was slain." He raised a single finger in the air. "I caught a glimpse of *one* of them. Then they…..disappeared."

The Krahl sighed in exasperation. "Like ghosts, I suppose, rising up from the blowing dust and then vanishing upon the wind." He assailed both men with his unwavering black eyes for a moment. "And not, of course, before carrying off every single scrap of Callimach's emblems. Everything. Right before the very eyes of all my noble soldiers." He turned around to address them all and raised his voice. "Is that the truth of it?" A silence followed throughout the wide courtyard and seemed to echo back from the tall, brooding figures of stone that surrounded them. Not a few glanced up uneasily at them.

"Robes, circlet…..and sword.," said the Krahl, *"And sword!"*

Udlass twisted himself in agony and Dafek cleared his throat again.

"But then they were spotted again, thank the Spirit," said the Krahl, looking once more at the touman-leader, a mock smile on his rugged face.

"Yes, Master," said Udlass, emphatically, "Some of my men saw the Mumblers hasten farther into the City and they followed them." He nodded his head. "They intended to capture them and bring them before my Master but….."

"But?"

The man quickly sank back into his painful and pathetic embarrassment. "My Master," he groaned, "they could not be caught. They could always be seen and followed but never caught. I do not know…..The Mumblers seemed to *fly!*"

"The Mumblers seemed to fly." The Krahl laughed, harshly. "And flew straight here."

The man nodded vigorously again and turned and pointed to the porticoed, stone building before which they stood.

The Krahl raised his eyes for the first time to the Shrine of Sammos.

"And you," he said in a low voice, after a while, to Udlass, "did not enter."

"Master," cried the touman-leader desperately, "I thought it best to – I went and reported to my own Master, Master Dafek. I posted men to stand guard."

"Noble men."

"Most noble men, Master."

The Krahl raised his arm. "Silence! This bleating is irritating my ears. Get out of my sight."

The man rose and scampered away.

The Odrum Master stood frowning up at the stone building. "Adjeek, Dafek, ad-Dura, and you - " he suddenly turned toward Sulcharek, who was standing nearby "walk with me. I want to show all of you something."

Leisurely, as if taking a stroll, they moved toward the east, toward the first row of alabaster statues that ringed the Shrine of Sammos. Sulcharek, being here before and glancing up at them, gave a shiver. He had never been over-fond of the place but now somehow it filled him with dread. "Do you see these figures, these heroic countenances?" asked the Krahl, indicating with a raised hand the closest statue. They all looked up at it.

Sulcharek saw by its base, with a jolt, that it was the likeness of Tasrich IX. "Master," he blurted, "this is the Emperor's very father."

The Krahl raised his eyes to the huge, blank eyes of the alabaster face. "Is it?" he said, lightly, as if remarking upon the weather. "Is it, indeed?"

He turned to them. "There is a right," he said, carefully and benignly, "given by the Divine to the Mundane. Oh, I was tutored as a boy by my own father in the ways of ancient wisdom, Great Men of Odrum, so do not be surprised by what I say. There is a right bestowed upon kings by gods." He spread his arms wide, indicating the place where they stood. "For a thousand years there has been such a right bestowed by the god of Sammar to the kings of Sammar and that right is given through a symbol; a symbol of the right to rule." The officers looked at each other and Sulcharek narrowed his eyes, trying to garner every nuance from the Krahl's rough face. "What is the symbol?" said the Krahl.

Something flashed through Sulcharek's mind and he gave a visible start.

A distant image of he and his father.....and a sword. *Yes? But what? Something –*

'When you are old enough and have learned to use your mind first, then I will give you a sword,' his father's voice echoed in his head. 'For all the great warriors of Sammar have done so before they got *their* swords.'

'Even the Emperor himself?' cried his own voice, a boy's voice.

'*Especially* the Emperor, for his sword is the very - '

".....right to rule," said Sulcharek aloud.

The Krahl turned toward the lone Sammkite who now stood within Sammar Gloria. "What did you say, Lordling Sulcharek?"

"The sword is the right to rule," said the young man. He went forward to the statue of Tasrich IX and pointed up at the stone sword grasped in his hand, directly at the graven image of Sammos's face upon its pommel.

The Krahl smiled.

The two men stood at the entrance to the Shrine of Sammos.

"Sulcharek of Pentes," said the one, "the Empire of Sammar has been conquered by my noble armies but Sammar is not mine. It cannot be mine unless you bring to me the sword of Callimach XI. It is the symbol of the right to rule this land. Given by the gods of this land. Somehow it is here. Bring it to me and you and your sons and your sons'

sons will rule over all Pentes for all time, second only to the Throne. This I swear before the World Spirit who now reigns in Sammar."

"I will," said the other.

Sulcharek held up the torch before himself in his left hand and brandished his sword in his right. *If those crazy priests want to jump me they had better think twice. No, they had better stay in their holy shadows and disappear for real.* If even one of them interfered, he would have no choice, would he? Even here within this place.

The air was cool and unpleasantly dank. *Do they catch pneumonia in here? How do they even survive?* He laughed out loud, scornfully. "Do we play a game now?" he chided the dark. "Hoping that the bad men will go away and that we will be able to keep all of our holy trinkets?"

The dark did not answer but instead threw his words back at him in great echoes. He swallowed and swept his torch slowly from side to side. "Probably a damned tunnel underneath this place anyway," he mumbled. Yet, he knew they were here. They had not departed. For there was a presence; unmistakeable. And deeper within.

In the end, he found what he sought.

It was indeed hidden. Hidden in plain sight.

By Sammos! Did they try to destroy it?

For what seemed an eternity, he stared down into the flames of the Altar, its light blinding him to all else inside the inner sanctum of the Shrine. Helplessly, he watched as the holy, untended fire licked its hungry, flaming tongues all about and around the sword of Callimach XI. It had been plunged into its depths. The tiny ruby eyes set in the face-shaped pommel gleamed up at him from the fire. *They gave it back. They gave it back, the fools. They tried to offer it back to.....*

Irresistibly, his eyes were drawn up, up to that giant stone figure which loomed over the Altar; up to its giant face.

Dimly, he was aware of both his bowels and his bladder letting go.

Sammos's giant eyes gleamed down at him, burning as red as the ones within the flames of the Altar.

He opened his mouth to scream.

"What insolence is this? What mockery?" thundered the Krahl when they brought him out to him.

"No mockery," gasped Adjeek, "I swear it, Master. We found him…..as he is. Upon the floor in front of the stone Altar."

"Did *they* do it to him?"

"There was no-one there, Master. Only shadows and dark and….. cold." The big man shivered. "When we saw him, we…..did not touch him but dragged him back out to you at once."

"Strange," murmured the Krahl. Then, after a brief pause, he stepped closer to the body of Sulcharek of Pentes and looked down at the face worked into the pommel of the sword that was plunged into the young man's breast. "But I suppose it is no matter now." He reached for the hilt.